How to Make RefrigerArt™

Refrigerators—they're not just for food anymore. They're for art, too!

And now you've got your very own sketchbook and fridge frame to get you started. Here's how to use RefrigerArt:

1. **Find the picture you want to complete.**
   Start at the beginning, in the middle, or at the end of the book—it doesn't matter! Just pick the image that you like! (The first half of the book has pictures to get you started, the second half has blank frames for you to draw within.)

2. **Get your pens, pencils, crayons—whatever you need—ready.**
   Draw the creature as you see it—as it looks in the real world, as it looks in your mind—however you want! Draw your brother with a rabbit's tail. Draw your best friend with a monkey tail. After all, everything's fair when it comes to your imagination.

3. **Place the finished picture in the magnetic frame.**
   You can just flip the book over and stick it in the slot, or tear the picture out first!

4. **"Hang" the picture on your fridge for everyone to see!**
   The magnetic back will keep it up.

5. **Repeat as necessary, and have fun drawing!**
   The frame can fit regular 8½-by-11-inch paper, so you can use it even when the book is finished!

Whose TAIL is this?

It's big and swishy.

But this creature's not a fishy.

It weighs a lot—might break your scale.

This giant mammal's called a <u>w</u>_____.

But don't take our word for it—

Draw whatever you see fit.

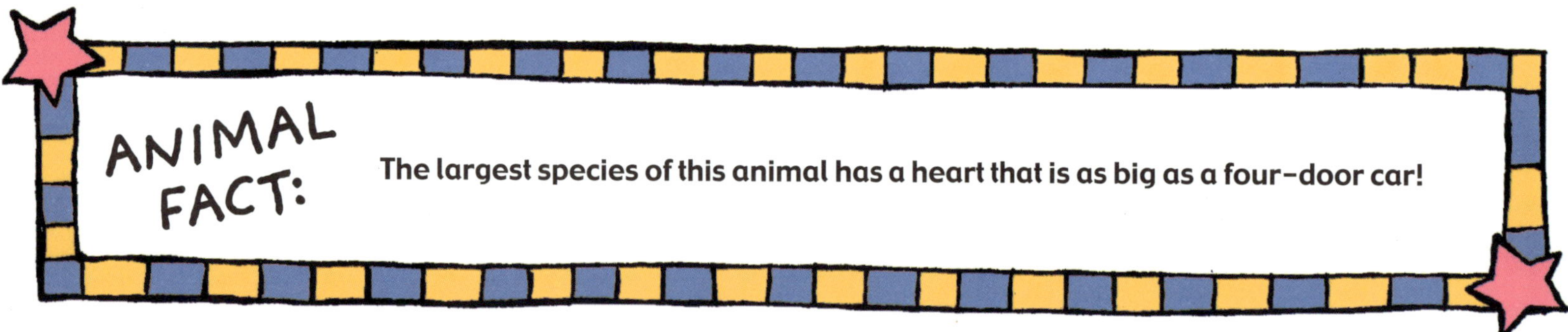

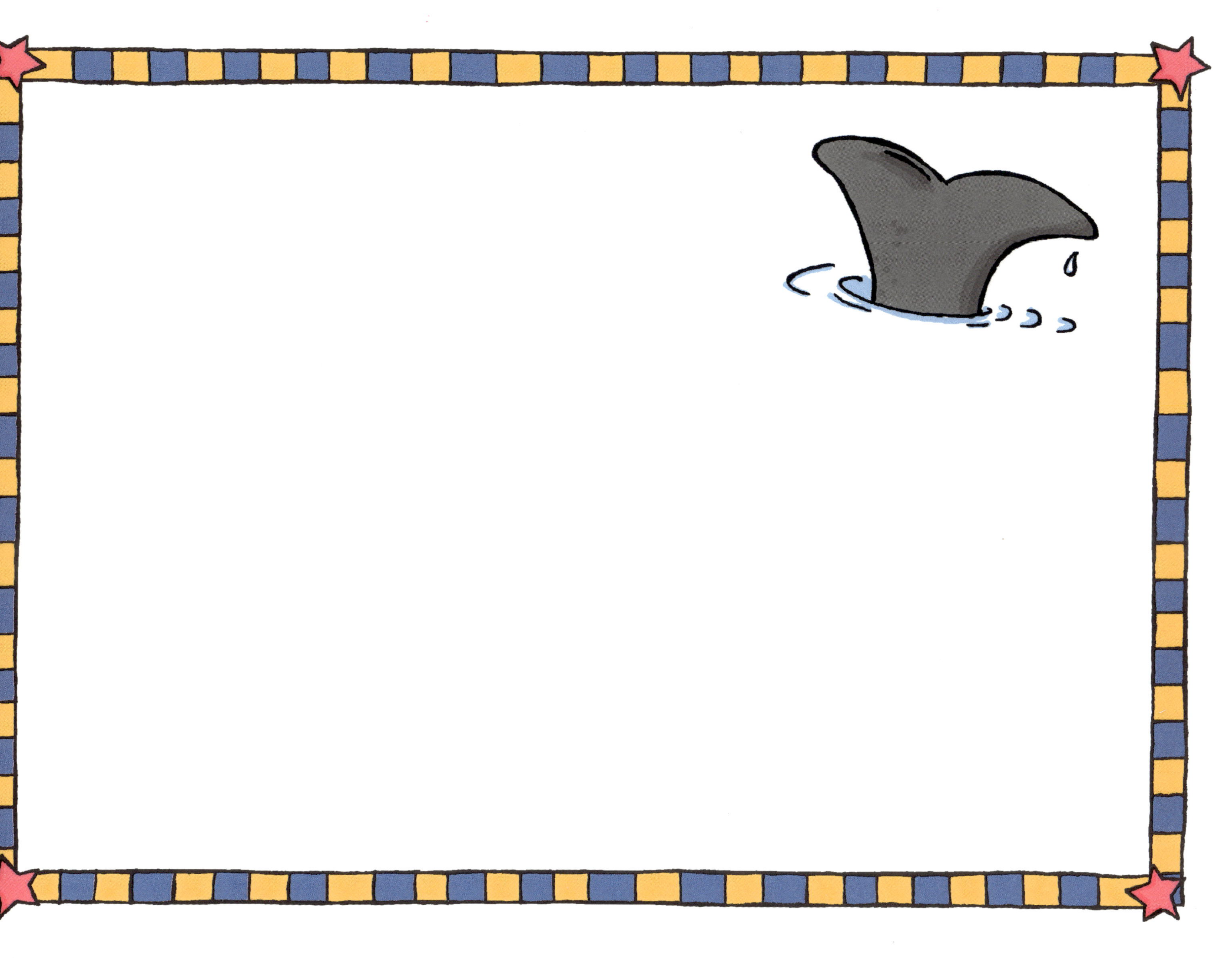

Whose TAIL is this?

This critter's small.

And it lives inside the wall!

You might have one in your house.

(We hope you don't, 'cause it's a M_____.)

Draw it small or draw it big.

Give it shoes, a hat, and wig!

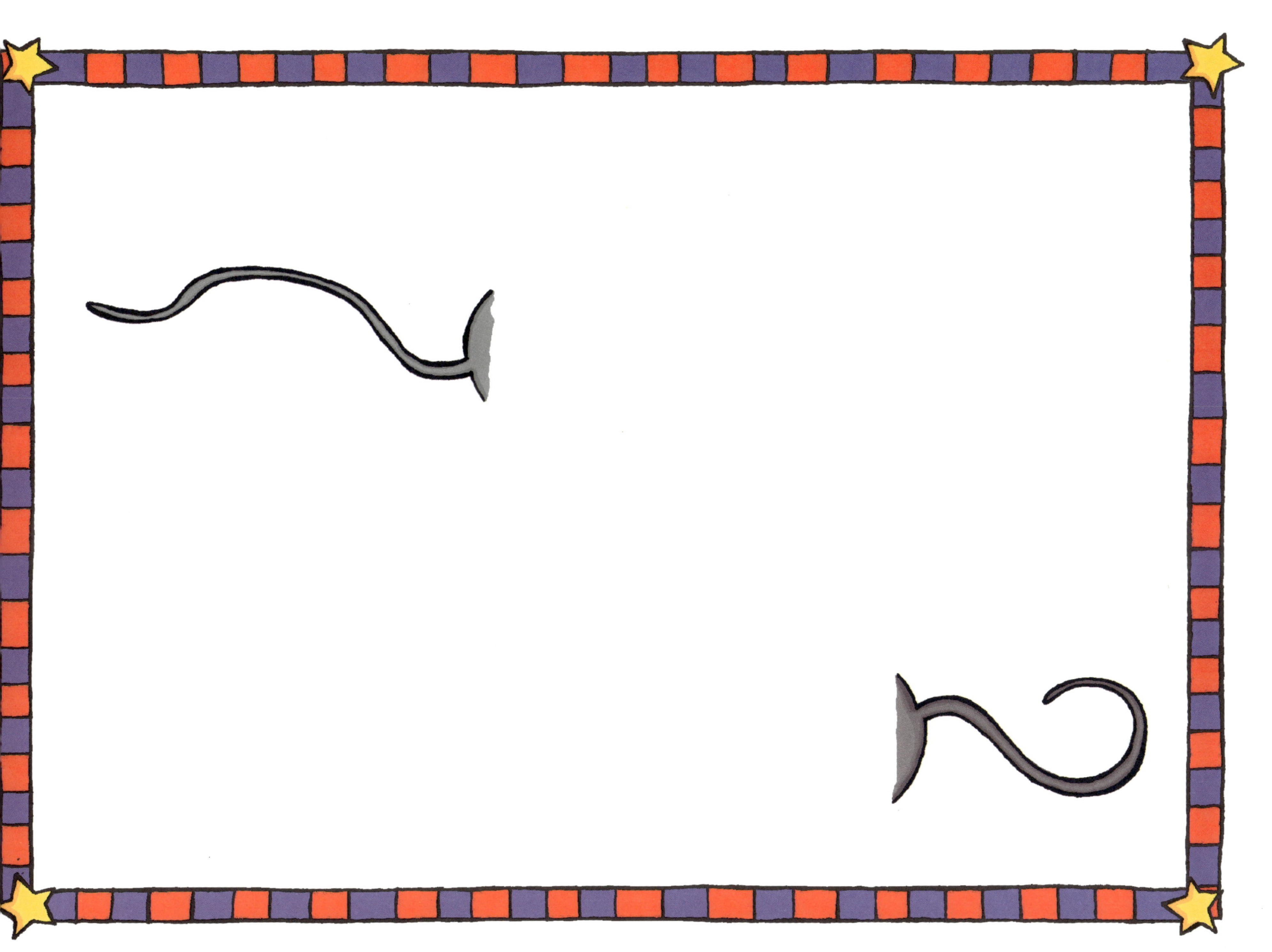

Whose TAIL is this?

It's white and fluffy.

Maybe it's a cat named Muffy?

It eats carrots as a habit.

And it hops—it's called a R_ _ _ _ _ _.

You can draw this funny creature

Or another with this feature.

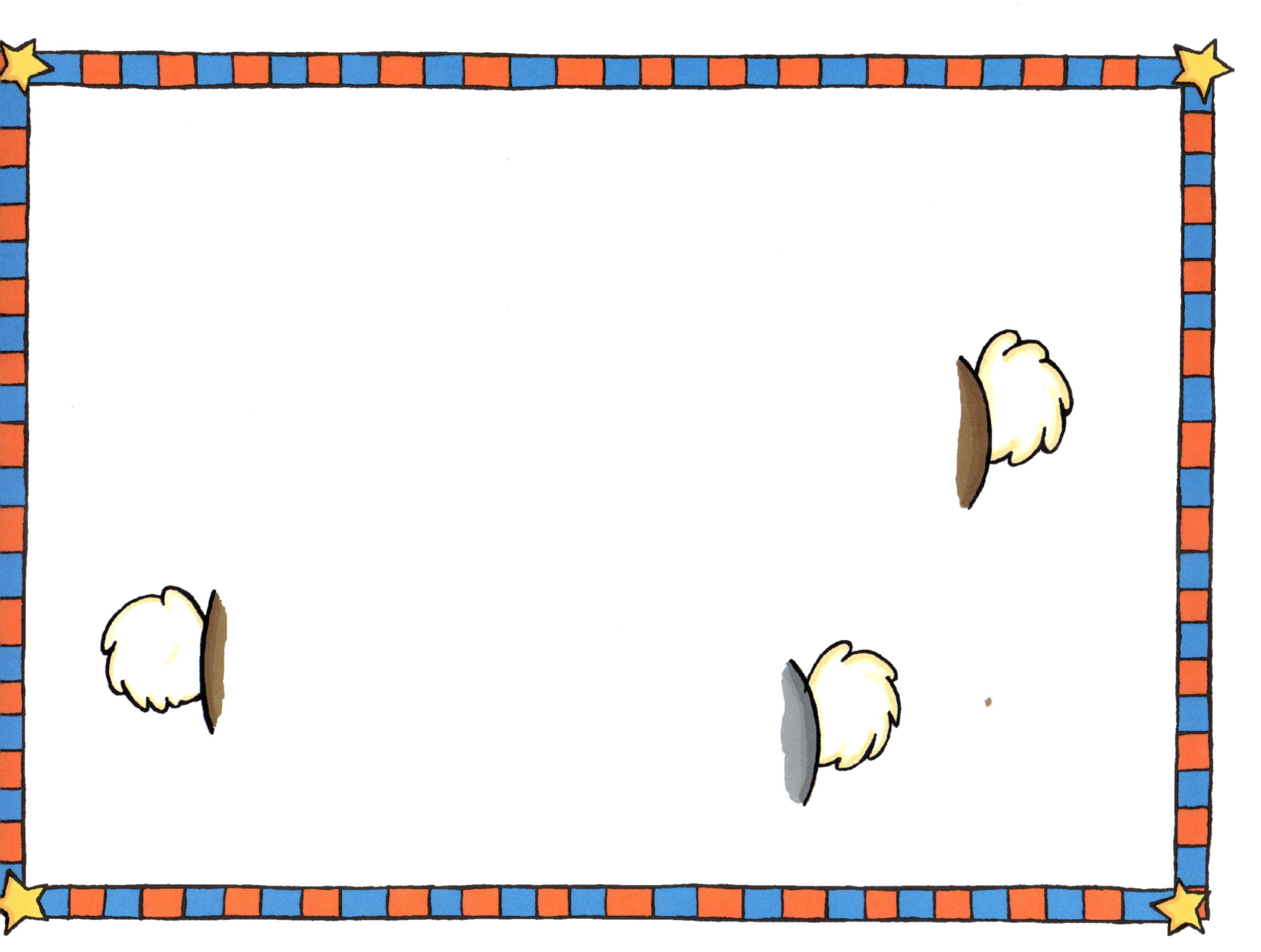

Whose TAIL is this?

It's bright and pretty.

You won't find it in the city.

If I were one, you'd hear me squawk,

"I'm proud to be a fine P _ _ _ _ _ _ _."

Draw this bird in all its beauty.

(After all, that is your duty.)

ANIMAL FACT: This creature's colorful train of feathers is supported by his actual tail. Usually the train lies flat, but when the male wants to show off to the female, he lifts it up into the air and struts around proudly.

Whose TAIL is this?

It hangs from trees.

For food? Bananas only, please.

It leaps and swings—it's very spunky.

Do you know it? It's a M_ _ _ _ _ _.

These creatures live deep in the jungle.

Draw them well—don't make a bungle.

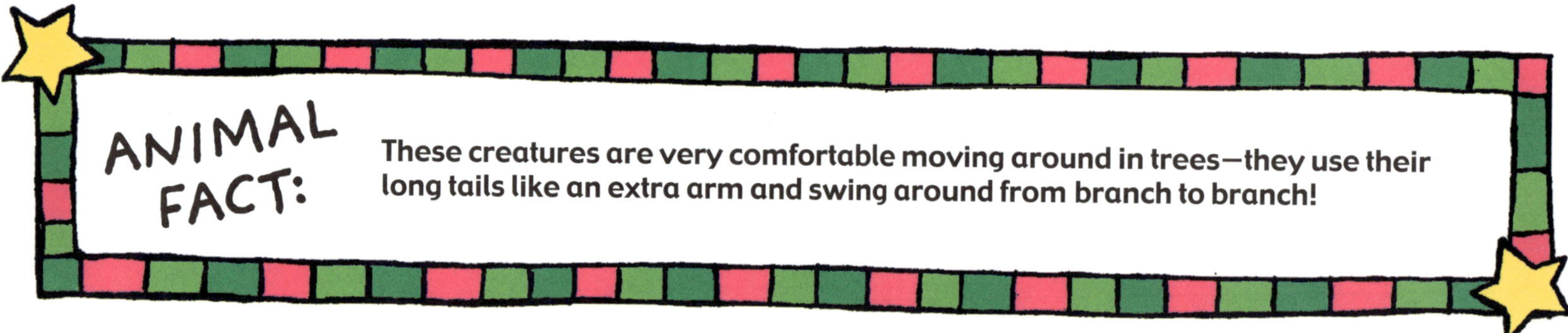

Whose TAIL is this?

It's very curly.

On the farm it wakes up early!

It loves the mud, and grows quite big!

Perhaps you know the oinking P _ _ ?

Another hint—this one eats slop.

Get drawing! Take it from the top!

Whose TAIL is this?

It's kind of long.

And this creature's very strong.

It kicks down doors with lots of force.

This creature gallops—it's a H_____.

You can draw it straight or silly.

Or, just draw a mare (or filly).

ANIMAL FACT: These creatures used to pull fire engines before cars were invented. Old firehouses have circular staircases because these animals figured out how to walk up straight ones!

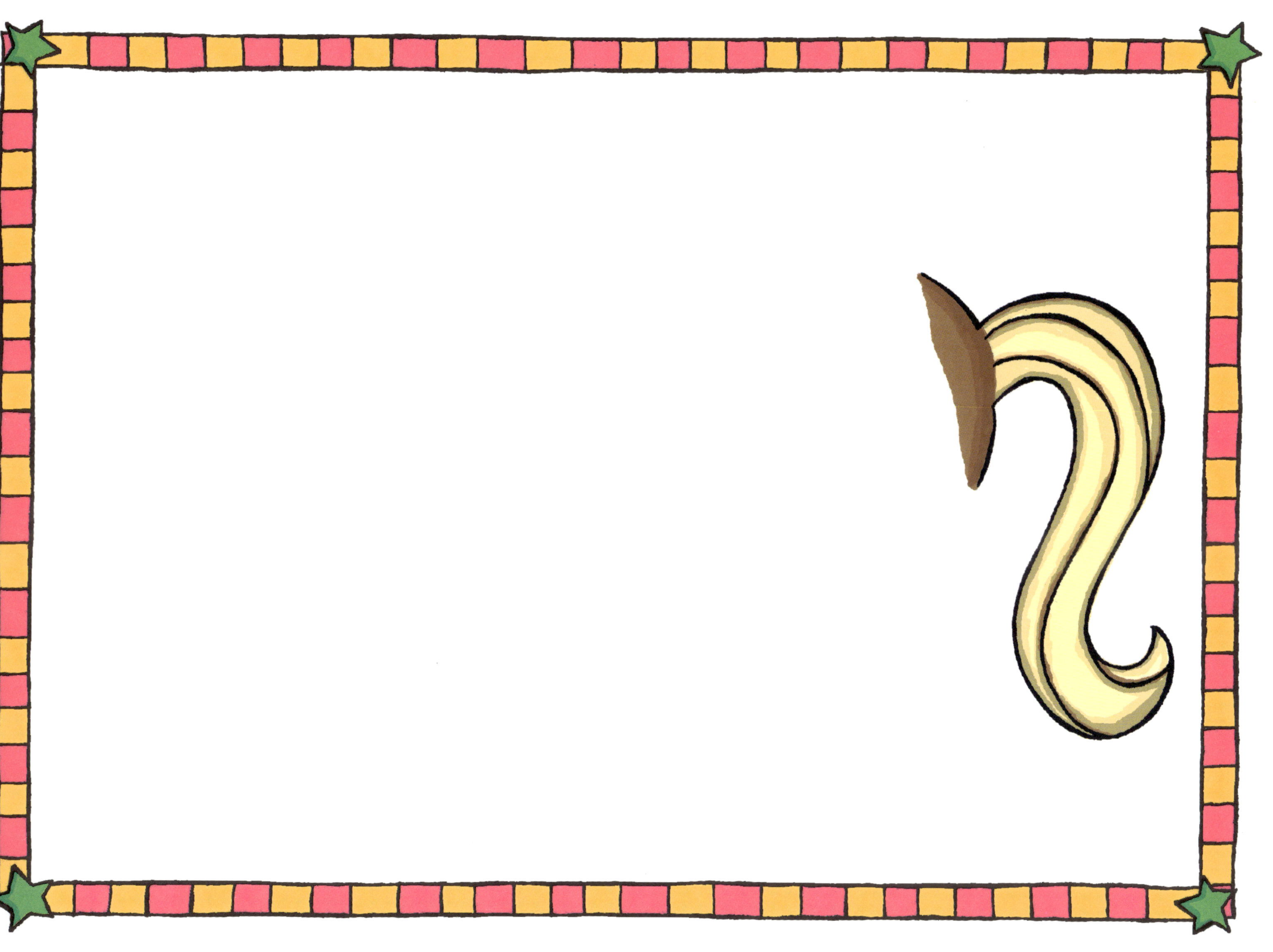

Whose TAIL is this?

It's hard to tell

Because it lives inside a shell.

This one moves slow—can't jump a hurdle.

Do you know it? It's a _Turtle_.

Here's one more hint: It lives in water.

Know it? If you don't, you oughtta.

Whose TAIL is this?

It smells quite ripe

And has a very special stripe.

When it gets scared it sprays out gunk.

This creature stinks. It's called a S _ _ _ _ _ .

If you see one, stay far away.

(You can draw it though, today.)

Whose TAIL is this?

It has big eyes.

And on the beach is where it lies.

It just eats fish for every meal.

And, it "arfs." It's called a <u>S</u> _ _ _ _.

Draw it big or draw it little!

Draw it playing on a fiddle!

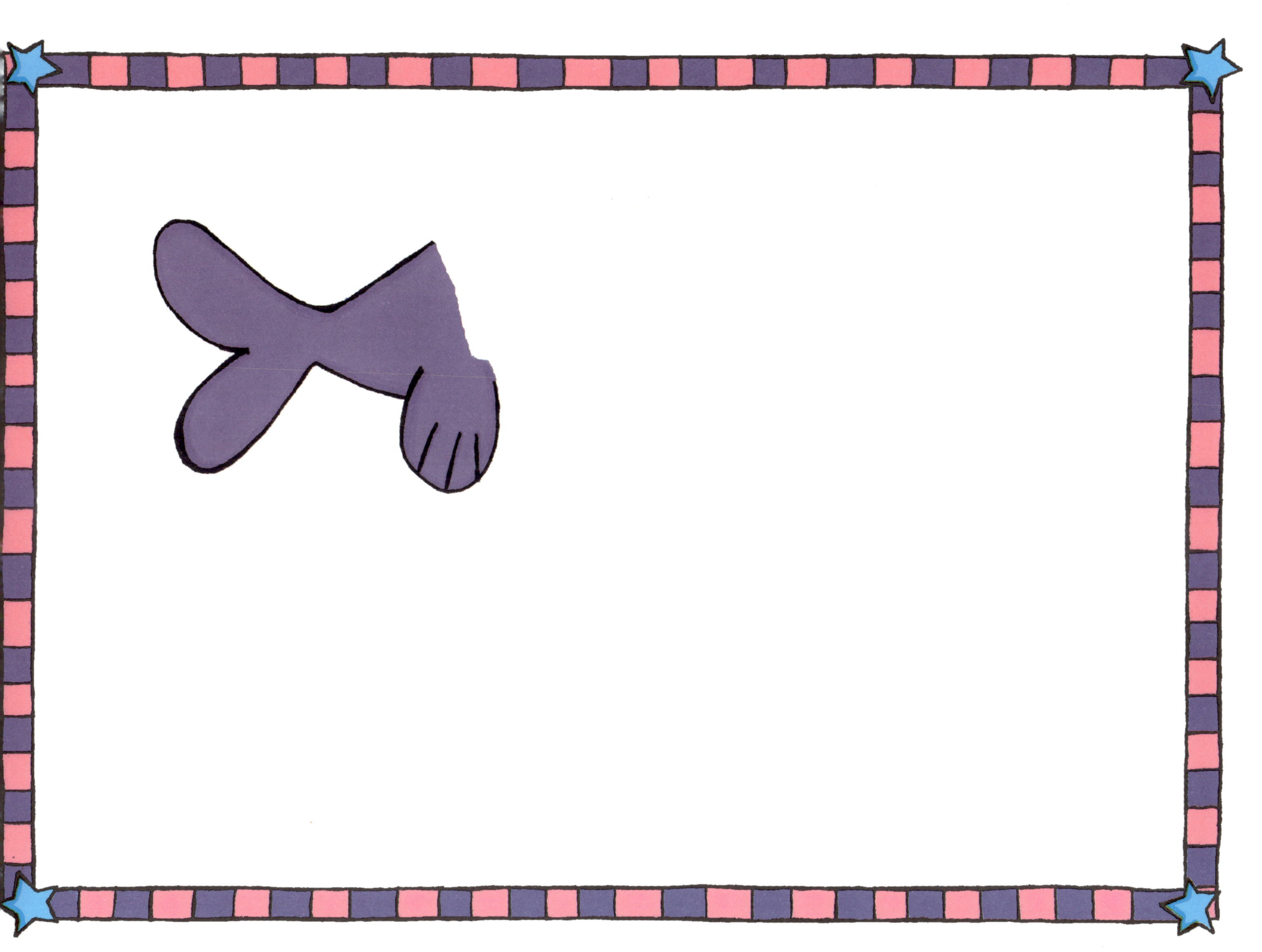

Whose TAIL is this?

This creature's "classic."

(It lived back in the Jurassic.)

Now it's gone—it lives no more.

You guessed it—it's a D_________.

This one ate trees deep in the forest

And called itself Apatosaurus!

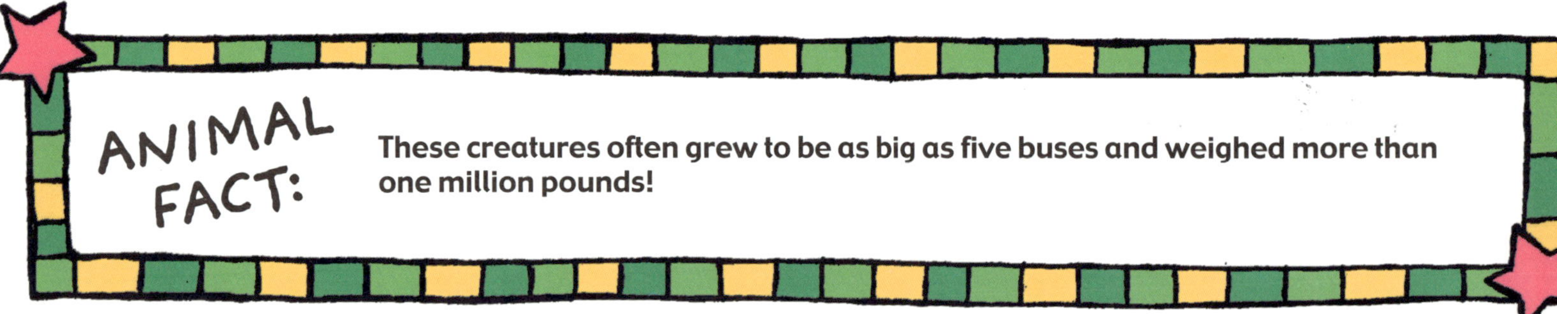

Whose TAIL is this?

It lives in oceans

And it swims with funny motions.

In trees it might be called a "treehorse."

But in seas it's called a S_________.

Draw it normal, draw it weird—

Draw it with a long, white beard!

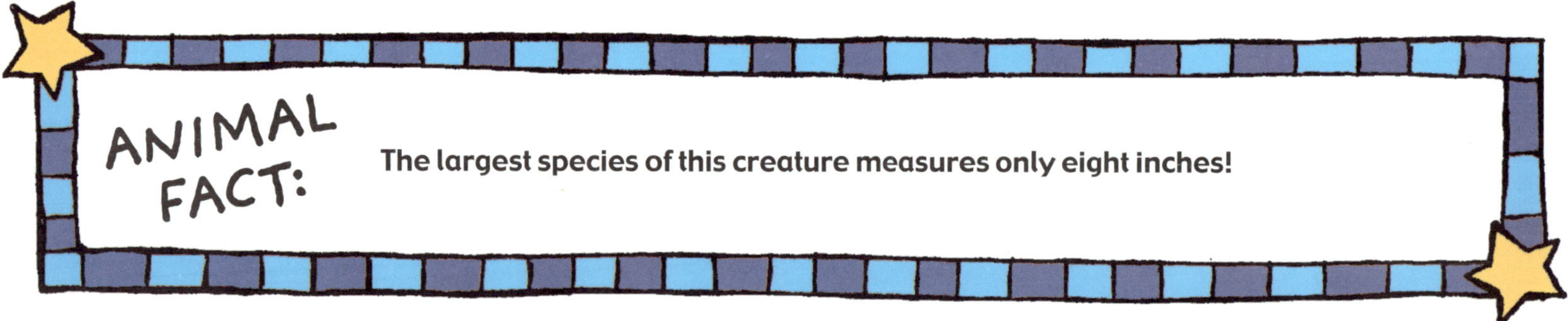

Whose TAIL is this?

You sure can tell—

This creature has an outer shell.

Don't be scared though—it's no mobster.

Perhaps you know it—it's a L _ _ _ _ _ _ .

One more thing: It's got two claws.

Now let your pen draw what it draws!

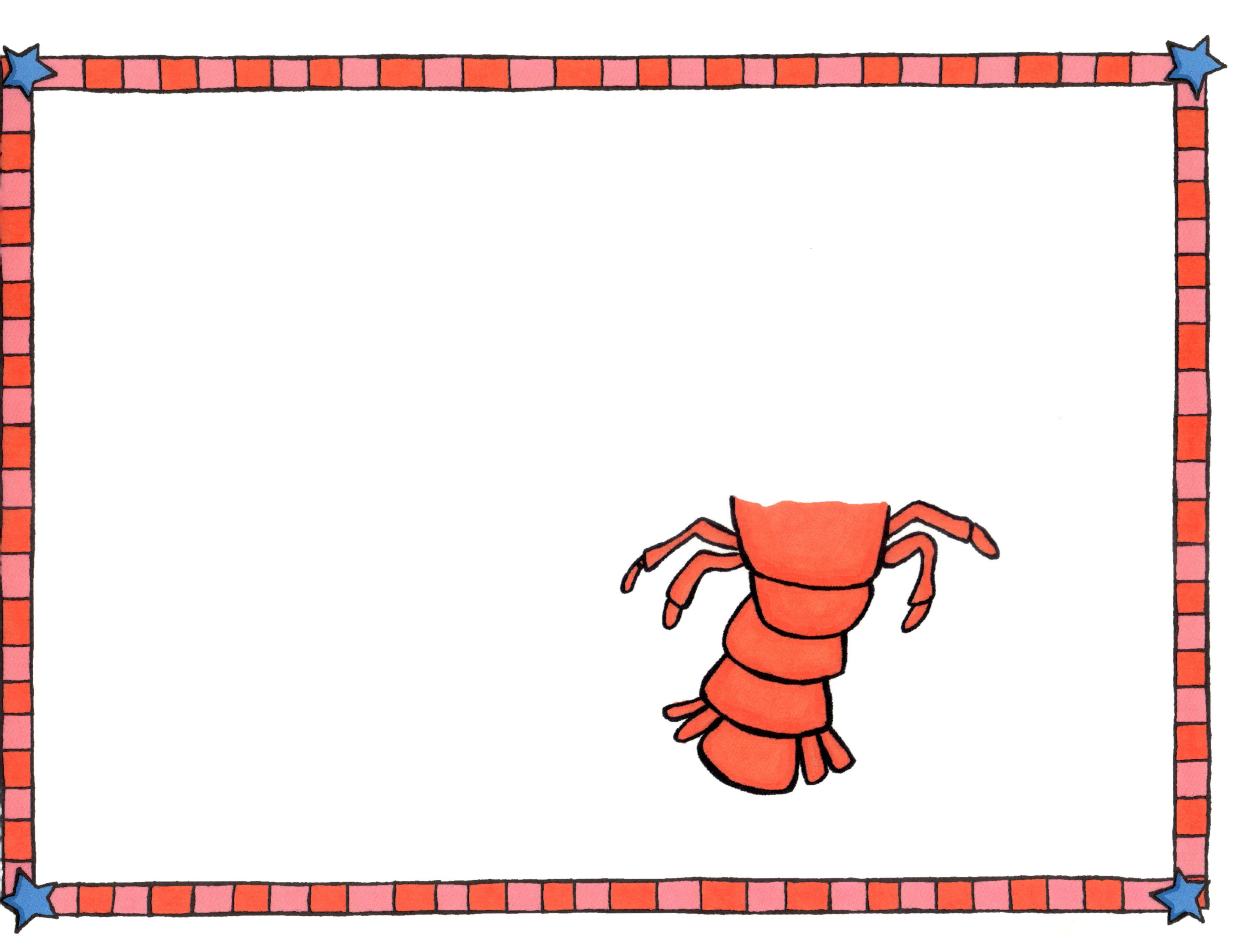

Whose TAIL is this?

This cat's got spots—
Not one or two, but lots and lots!
It kind of looks like it's been peppered.
Now you know that it's a L _ _ _ _ _ _ _.
Or it might be something crazy.
Draw it, if you don't feel lazy.

ANIMAL FACT:

All kinds of these creatures are spotted, even the black ones (sometimes called black panthers). And no two of them have the same spot pattern.

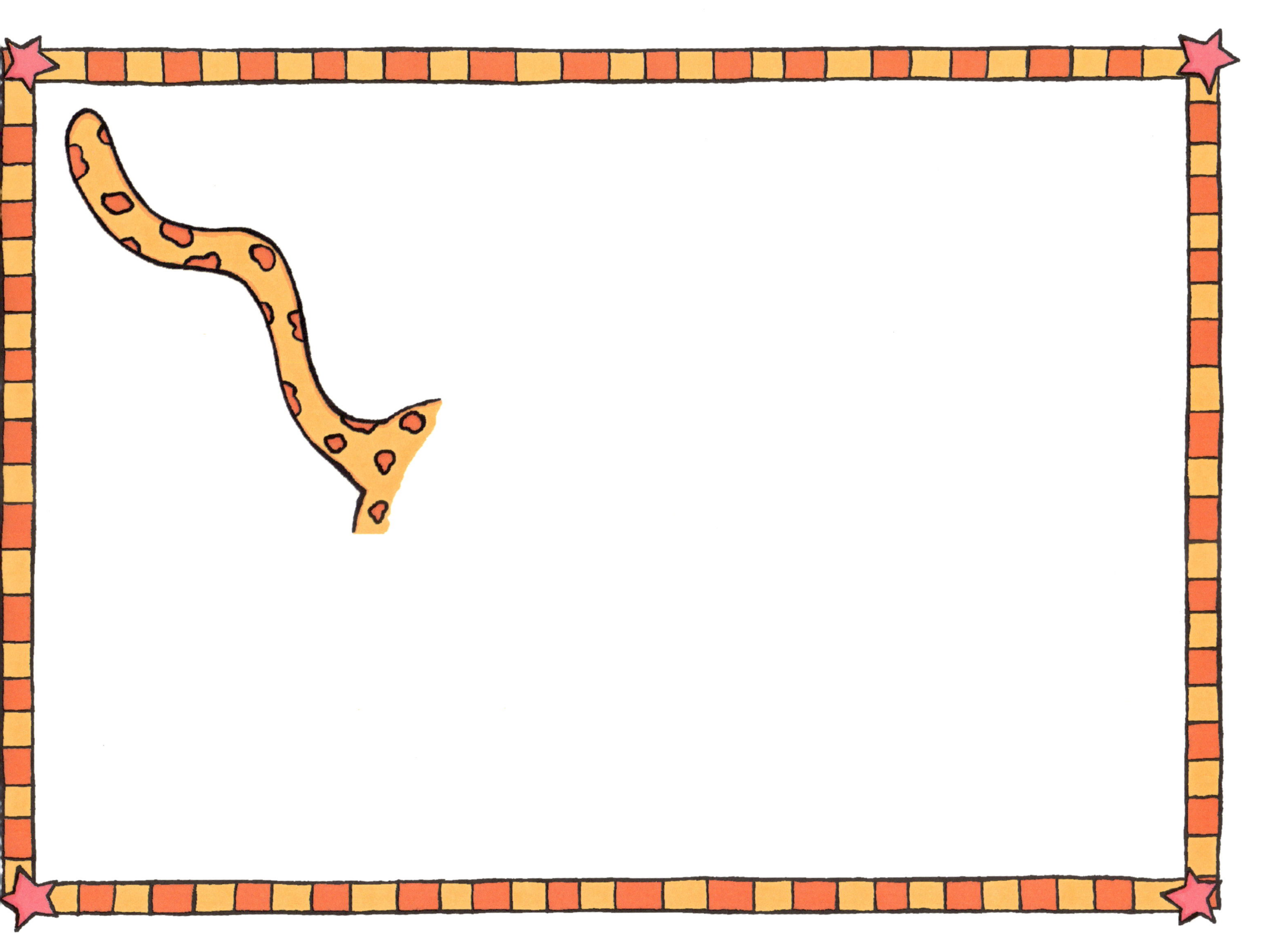

Whose TAIL is this?

It's got a rattle,

Warning when it's time for battle.

This reptile can make us quake.

It slithers and it's called a S_____.

Draw this creature—draw another!

Draw your dog (or little brother).

Draw whatever you want, and then

Just turn the page, and draw again!

ANIMAL FACT: These creatures are cold blooded (they only absorb the temperature around them—they don't have a regular body temperature like we do). So in the winter, they cuddle together for warmth!

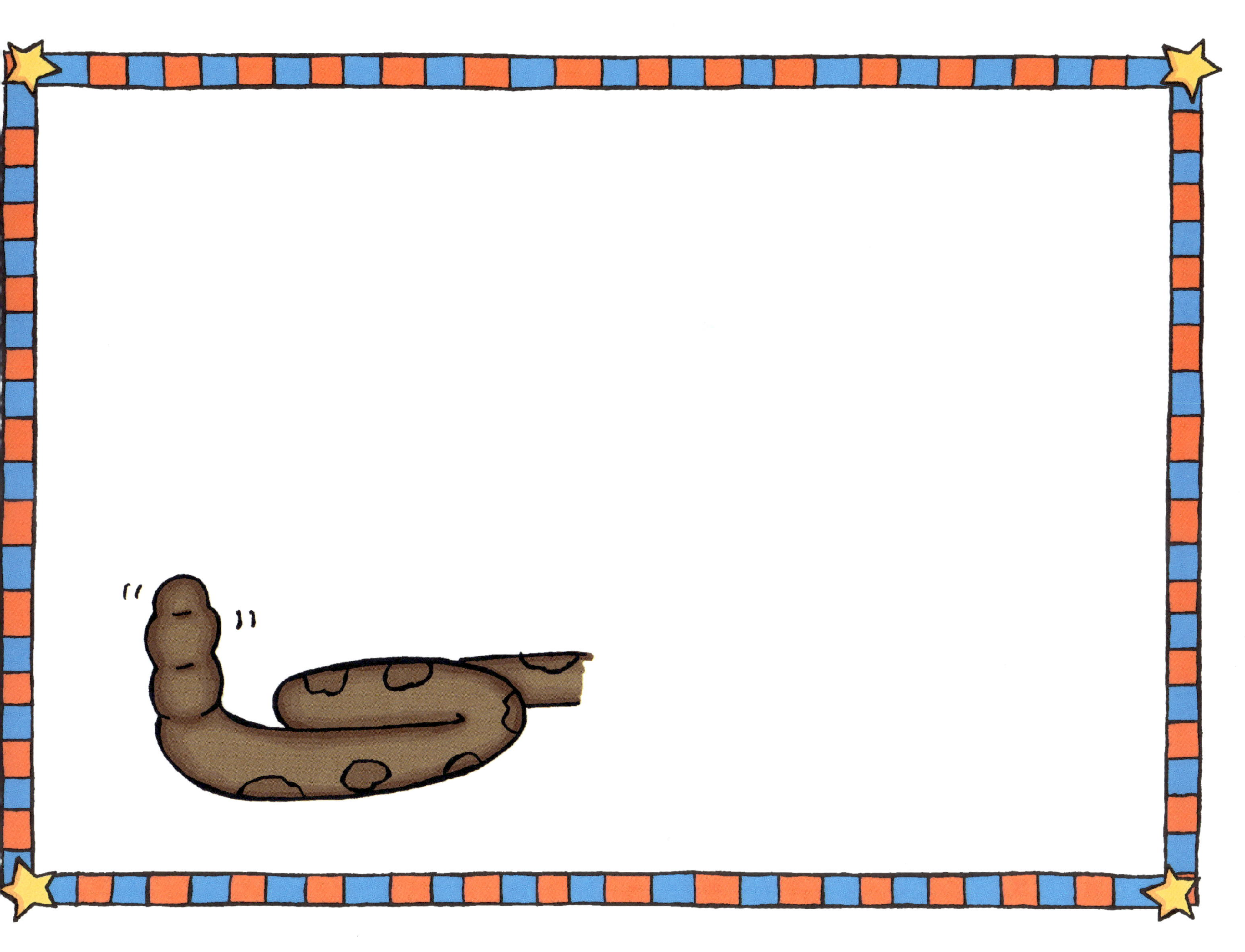

I LoVE

YoU

SAVANNAH